Meet the Robinsons: The Movie Storybook
Copyright © 2007 Disney Enterprises, Inc.
RADIO FLYER is a registered trademark of Radio Flyer Inc. and is used with permission.
Printed in the United States of America.

For information address HarperCollins Children's Books, a division of HarperCollins Publishers,
1350 Avenue of the Americas, New York, NY 10019.
www.harpercollinschildrens.com

ISBN-10: 0-06-112476-1 — ISBN-13: 978-0-06-112476-1
❖
First Edition

DISNEY
MEET THE ROBINSONS

THE MOVIE STORYBOOK

Adapted by Barbara Bazaldua
Illustrated by the Disney Storybook Artists
Designed by Tony Fejeran of Disney Publishing's Global Design Group

HarperEntertainment
An Imprint of HarperCollinsPublishers

Late one cold and rainy night, a young woman wearing a hooded cloak hurried toward the 6th Street Orphanage. She laid a box down on the front steps of the brick building.

Inside, Mildred, the kindhearted orphanage director, heard a knock at the door. But when she peeked outside, she saw no one . . . until she looked down. There, in the box at her feet, was a tiny newborn baby. Tenderly, Mildred carried the infant boy inside, out of the dark, cold night.

Twelve years later, Lewis still lived at the 6th Street Orphanage. He had become a smart, curious boy who could invent almost anything. But he couldn't invent what he wanted most: a family.

Lewis had met with many possible parents, but something always seemed to go wrong. The day he decided to show off his new Peanut-Butter-and-Jelly Sandwich Maker, the machine went berserk, squirting peanut butter and jelly everywhere! The couple left abruptly . . . without Lewis.

Near tears, Lewis ran to the roof to be alone. Mildred followed and tried to cheer him up, but Lewis was too upset.

"My own mother didn't want me," he sighed.

"Maybe she wanted you but couldn't take care of you," Mildred replied.

Her words gave Lewis an idea. He was just a baby when he saw her last, but he knew her image was in his brain somewhere. If a machine scanned his brain for the image, then he'd find his mother and they would be a family!

Lewis immediately went to work on his invention. He did research and drew lots of plans, and then he welded, hammered, and sawed.

Night after night, Lewis's noisy work kept his poor roommate, Mike "Goob" Yagoobian, awake.

At last, early in the morning of the school science fair, Lewis put the finishing touches on his invention. He called it the Memory Scanner.

Meanwhile, a very tired Goob headed out for his championship baseball game, hoping he could keep his eyes open.

At the science fair, there were three judges: Mr. Willerstein (Lewis's science teacher), the school coach, and Dr. Krunklehorn (a special guest scientist from Inventco). They watched as the students set up their projects.

Lewis hurried to his table. His project was covered with a blanket so it would be a surprise for the judges.

Swiftly he unloaded the blanket-covered invention and lifted it onto the table. Suddenly a strange boy reached out from the blanket and yanked Lewis underneath.

Huddled next to Lewis's invention, the mysterious boy introduced himself, "Special Agent Wilbur Robinson of the TCTF."

"The what?" asked the bewildered Lewis.

"Time Continuum Task Force," said Wilbur. He explained that he was from the future and he had come to protect Lewis from a tall man in a bowler hat.

Lewis thought the strange kid was, well, strange.

Wilbur ducked out from under the blanket and looked around. Suddenly he thought he spotted the bad guy! Wilbur tackled the "suspect." But it was just a boy carrying a model of the solar system. Oops!

Wilbur didn't see the real Bowler Hat Guy, who was sneaking across the other side of the gym. The bowler hat—which was actually a robot named Doris—flew up off Bowler Hat Guy's head and over to Lewis's invention. Unseen, Doris loosened some of the invention's bolts and sneaked away on her metallic legs.

Lewis's big moment had arrived. Proudly, he stood before the judges and uncovered his project—the Memory Scanner.

Lewis told them his invention could help people remember the past. Lewis was excited—in a few seconds he'd turn on the machine and remember his mother. Then he could find her, and they would become a family.

When Lewis turned on the Memory Scanner, the machine didn't work as planned. It started to shake. The fan on top flew upward, hitting the lights, which set off the gym sprinklers and ruined all the other science projects. The science fair was a complete mess!

Lewis watched helplessly as kids and teachers ran out the doors. Upset, he fled the room alone.

When everyone else was gone, Bowler Hat Guy crept out from his hiding place. He and Doris stole the Memory Scanner.

Lewis went back to the orphanage roof and furiously ripped pages out of his invention notebook. But when he flung the crumpled drawing of the Memory Scanner away, it came bouncing back. Lewis looked up and could see Wilbur, trying to hide behind a brick wall.

"Coo coo!" Wilbur warbled, pretending to be a pigeon.

Lewis rolled his eyes. "What are you doing up here?" he asked.

Wilbur quickly tried to explain things to Lewis. "I really am from the future. And there really is this Bowler Hat Guy," Wilbur said. "He stole a Time Machine, came to the science fair, and ruined your project!"

Lewis didn't buy it. "My project didn't work because I'm no good," he snapped. "You're not from the future! You're crazy!"

"If I prove to you I'm from the future, will you go back to the science fair?" Wilbur asked.

Lewis agreed. Then Wilbur pushed him off the roof! Lewis fell through the air, yelling, until—*thunk!* He landed on something in midair.

Wilbur jumped down beside Lewis and pushed a button. A sleek, shiny machine appeared around them and blasted off into space.

"Where are we going?" Lewis shouted.

"To the future!" Wilbur exclaimed.

All of a sudden, they burst through a bubble of light as colors swirled around them. When Lewis looked out of the window, everything had changed. Tall buildings gleamed below. People soared past in flying vehicles. He was in the future!

"With this Time Machine, you can take me back in time to see my mom!" Lewis exclaimed.

Wilbur reminded Lewis that he had agreed to return to the science fair. They started to argue, and Lewis tried to grab the Time Machine controls. In the struggle, the Time Machine plunged to the ground! Dizzy but unhurt, the boys stared at the wrecked machine.

"You have to fix it," Wilbur said.

"Only if you promise to take me to see my mom," Lewis replied.

Wilbur reluctantly agreed. "Deal," he said.

Meanwhile, Bowler Hat Guy and Doris went straight from the science fair to Inventco. Bowler Hat Guy proudly showed off the Memory Scanner, telling everyone it was his own invention—except he didn't know how it worked! Luckily Doris hovered outside the window, holding up cue cards for the silly villain, trying to explain how to operate the machine.

But then the chairman lowered the window blinds. No more cue cards! Bowler Hat Guy was on his own.

Trying very, very hard to be smart, Bowler Hat Guy took the headset attached to the machine, and put it onto the head of the Inventco chairman. But then he didn't know how to turn it on! He pressed so many different buttons that the Memory Scanner crashed to the floor and broke. As it fell, the headset wires dragged the chairman across the table and onto the floor.

Bowler Hat Guy was tossed out of the building. The Memory Scanner quickly followed.

"We must find that boy!" shouted Bowler Hat Guy. He knew Lewis was the only person who could make the Memory Scanner work.

In the future, Wilbur and Lewis were pushing the wrecked Time Machine into the Robinsons' garage. Wilbur grabbed a silly fruit hat and plopped it on Lewis's head to hide his yellow spiky hair. Wilbur said he didn't want anyone to know Lewis was from the past.

"Your hair's a dead giveaway," Wilbur explained. "Stay here." Wilbur went to get the Time Machine's blueprints from Carl, the family robot.

Carl had seen Lewis arrive with Wilbur, and he was freaked out. "Bringing him here could alter the entire time stream!" he cried.

But Wilbur stayed cool. "Wilbur Robinson never fails!" Wilbur said. He just had to convince Lewis to fix the Time Machine, return to the past, and repair the Memory Scanner.

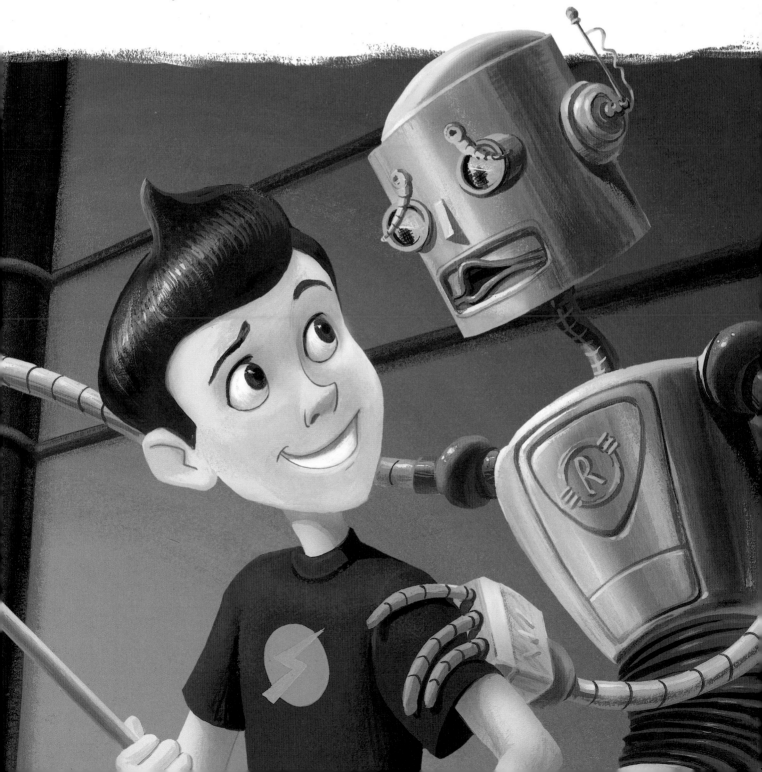

Back in the garage, Lewis accidentally walked under a Travel Tube and was sucked up into it. He popped out onto the front lawn and met a funny old man who wore his clothes backwards. It was Grandpa Bud, looking for his teeth.

"I need to get back to the garage," Lewis told Grandpa. "Wilbur left me there, and I wasn't supposed to leave."

Grandpa said he knew a shortcut, so they set off through the house. Along the way, Lewis saw many strange things.

They passed through the train room, where Uncle Gaston raced Aunt Billie's enormous toy train by shooting himself out of a cannon.

They watched Uncle Art blast off to make an intergalactic pizza delivery. They saw Cousin Laszlo zip overhead in his helicopter helmet, splashing paint on Cousin Tallulah's skyscraper hat. They saw Uncle Fritz arguing with his hand-puppet wife, Petunia. They even found Grandma dancing happily by herself. But they didn't find Grandpa Bud's lost teeth—or the garage.

When they opened the last door, a blast of music greeted them.

"That's Wilbur's mom, Franny," said Grandpa. Franny was conducting a band of frogs!

"We need someone on maracas!" Franny called.

Soon Lewis was shaking the maracas and having a ball! He even spotted one of the frogs wearing Grandpa's teeth. The Robinsons were different—but they were fun!

When Lewis finally got back to the Robinsons' garage, Wilbur was already there. They studied the Time Machine blueprints. "What if I can't fix it?" Lewis asked.

Wilbur told Lewis about his dad, Cornelius Robinson. Cornelius was an inventor who never gave up, even when he failed. He was called the Founder of the Future, and his motto was "Keep moving forward."

"Dude, I can't take you seriously in that hat." Wilbur switched Lewis's fruit hat for a baseball cap.

Inspired, Lewis started to work on the Time Machine. Hours later, he thought he was done. But when they tested the machine, it broke again!

At dinner, Lewis couldn't help feeling sad. After all, he had failed again.

The family started asking Lewis friendly questions. Wilbur couldn't let them find out that Lewis was from the past, or he would be in big trouble. So he distracted everyone by starting a meatball fight!

Instantly, the air was thick with flying meatballs. Gaston shot them at Franny, who karate chopped them away. The family cheered with delight.

Meanwhile, Bowler Hat Guy and Doris searched for Lewis at the orphanage. Instead of Lewis, they found Goob. Poor Goob had fallen asleep during his game, missed the winning catch, and lost the championship. His teammates had clobbered him and given him a black eye. "Mr. Steak, you're my only friend" he said miserably to the piece of meat he was holding over his eye.

Bowler Hat Guy gave Goob some very bad advice: "Everyone will tell you to let go and move on, but don't! Instead, let it fester and boil inside of you!"

Goob sighed and said Lewis might be on the roof.

A clue on the orphanage rooftop led Bowler Hat Guy and Doris to the future. Soon they were lurking outside the Robinsons' house.

Doris gave Bowler Hat Guy a smaller version of herself. It was Little Doris. Then both hats flew toward the house.

Bowler Hat Guy delightedly watched everything through Little Doris's mini camera. He had to find a way to get Lewis!

During dinner, Carl made sandwiches with a machine that looked just like Lewis's own Peanut-Butter-and-Jelly Sandwich Maker. "Where did he get that?" Lewis wondered.

When the machine jammed, Wilbur and his family asked Lewis to fix it. But when he turned the machine back on, it exploded, covering everything in peanut butter and jelly.

"You failed!" Grandpa Bud exclaimed, delighted.

"From failing you learn," Aunt Billie explained. "From success? Mmm—not so much."

Lewis realized the Robinsons didn't think failure was bad. It just meant you could—and should—try again. The next attempt would be better!

Suddenly the ground shook. The walls trembled. *Crash!* A Tyrannosaurus rex, controlled by Little Doris on its head, smashed through the window and snatched Lewis. Bowler Hat Guy had used the Time Machine to go back through time and get a dinosaur!

The Robinson family flew into action. Gaston fired meatballs. Uncle Joe and Tallulah stretched out Carl to trip the giant beast. Laszlo squirted paint on it. Franny used karate moves. Uncle Art blasted pizza dough. Finally, Wilbur helped Lewis escape from the dinosaur's grasp.

But then the dino snatched Wilbur instead! Lewis grabbed a shovel, jumped into the dinosaur's mouth, and jammed the shovel between its teeth.

As the boys held on to the shovel and dangled over the dino's gaping throat, Wilbur saw Gaston's cannon stuck in its teeth. He yanked it free and blasted Little Doris off the dino's head. The T. rex collapsed.

Victory for the Robinsons!

The Robinsons gathered around Lewis and Wilbur. Lewis couldn't believe they had been willing to put themselves at risk just to save him.

"You are a very special kid," declared Uncle Art.

"What do you say, Lewis? Do you want to be a Robinson?" asked Franny.

Lewis was shocked! Finally he had a family!

But Carl was nervous. It was time for Wilbur to explain everything.

Wilbur grabbed Lewis's hat. The family saw the yellow spiky hair and gasped!

"I'm sorry," Franny said. "You have to go back to your own time."

Lewis didn't understand.

"Can I at least go back and find my mom?" he asked. "Wilbur promised."

Franny turned to Wilbur. "You promised what?!"

"I was never gonna do it!" Wilbur said, guiltily.

Lewis had heard enough. It was the worst rejection yet. Wilbur had lied to him. Lewis ran off in tears.

Lewis was so upset that he did not run away when Bowler Hat Guy suddenly appeared in the stolen Time Machine. He and Doris had heard everything.

"We arc offering you a deal," Bowler Hat Guy told Lewis. "We'll take you back to find your mommy, and you fix the Memory Scanner."

Lewis saw this as his only hope to meet his mother and have a family, so he climbed into the Time Machine.

Wilbur ran after him. But it was too late. Wilbur watched Lewis and Bowler Hat Guy disappear into the night. He had to do something!

Bowler Hat Guy flew Lewis beyond the futuristic city to his hideaway—the old orphanage!

Lewis repaired the Memory Scanner, but Bowler Hat Guy did not take Lewis back in time to see his mother. Instead, he ordered Doris to tie up Lewis!

Then Bowler Hat Guy ripped off his cape, revealing a frayed, filthy, and much-too-small baseball uniform.

"It is I—Mike Yagoobian!" he shouted.

"Goob?! How'd you end up like this?" Lewis exclaimed.

"Because of you, I fell asleep and missed the winning catch!" Bowler Hat Guy said. "You ruined my life!"

Goob's bitterness over one lost baseball game had kept people from adopting him. So he had stayed at the orphanage his whole life, feeling more and more jealous as Lewis became successful.

Then Goob met Doris, a rejected invention of Robinson Industries, and together, they stole the Time Machine and traveled to the past to ruin Lewis's future.

Lewis finally understood. If he returned to his time in the past, Lewis himself would grow up to be Cornelius Robinson, Wilbur's dad!

"Now I'll return to Inventco, pass the Memory Scanner off as mine, and ruin your future!" said Bowler Hat Guy as he hauled Lewis and the Memory Scanner to the roof.

Suddenly Lewis heard Wilbur's signal: "Coo coo!" Wilbur and Carl were high up in the air thanks to Carl's robot legs, which could stretch to make him really tall.

Lewis shoved the Memory Scanner off the roof and jumped into Carl's outstretched arms.

Doris and Bowler Hat Guy got into the Time Machine and followed the trio toward the Robinsons' home. Suddenly Doris shot a grappling hook at Carl and snatched the Memory Scanner. As she and Bowler Hat Guy blasted back into the past, Bowler Hat Guy shouted "Take a good look around you, boys, because your future is about to change!"

Wilbur and Lewis were horrified. Carl was injured and now they were stuck with nothing but the broken Time Machine. The entire future was at risk!

Wilbur pleaded with Lewis to fix the Time Machine. But Lewis didn't think he could do it.

"Lewis! Lewis!" Wilbur pleaded, but his voice started to fade. Then a swirling black cloud appeared in the sky, and Wilbur disappeared into it!

Why? Because, back in Lewis's time, Bowler Hat Guy had sold the Memory Scanner to Inventco as his own invention. As he signed the contract with Inventco, the future was changing!

Lewis raced back to the Robinsons' house and ran inside. He yelled for the family, but no one answered.

Something that looked like an evil version of Lewis's Memory Scanner was showing Doris's memories of how she had created this horrible future! It was Doris who was the evil one all along!

Then the Robinsons appeared and began walking toward him. They looked cruel, and all of them wore bowler hats! They were under Doris's control!

Lewis went to the garage, jumped into the Time
Machine, and began working frantically to fix it. His
hands shook as he connected wires, turned knobs, and
flipped switches.

At last Lewis was finished. Gasping, he pressed a button. The Time Machine roared to life, and Lewis shot out from the garage!

He zoomed through swarms of attacking bowler hats, then swerved into a tunnel. A giant hat blocked the exit at the other end.

Quickly, Lewis flipped switches on the Time Machine's control panel. He wanted to return to one specific time and place.

Lewis and the Time Machine suddenly appeared in the Inventco boardroom, where Bowler Hat Guy was signing his name.

"Goob! Stop!" Lewis shouted.

"What—what are you doing?" asked Bowler Hat Guy.

Gesturing toward Doris, Lewis said, "She's using you, Goob, and once she gets what she wants, she'll get rid of you."

When Bowler Hat Guy learned how Doris would ruin the entire future, he tore up the contract. Furious, Doris attacked Lewis.

"I am never going to invent you," Lewis yelled. And with that, Doris disappeared. Forever.

Without Doris, Bowler Hat Guy was just Goob. He went with Lewis to the future.

Before their very eyes, they saw Doris's dark, evil future turn bright and happy again—into the future that Cornelius Robinson had created.

They landed on the Robinsons' lawn, and Wilbur tackled Goob before Lewis explained that Goob wasn't a bad guy anymore. While Lewis and Wilbur talked, Goob quietly walked away. It was time for him to find his own future.

The rest of the Robinsons came out of the house, and Lewis happily ran to them. That's when Cornelius came home. He and Lewis recognized each other at once!

Franny pointed to Wilbur as the troublemaker, but Cornelius didn't mind. He showed Lewis his lab, including the Memory Scanner. It really had worked, after all!

"So this will be my future?" Lewis asked.

"If you make the right choices and keep moving forward," Cornelius replied. "You need to get back to that science fair and find out for yourself."

Wilbur and Lewis climbed into the Time Machine.
"We'll see you soon!" the Robinsons called.

Once the Time Machine was in the air, Wilbur did
something unexpected.

"We agreed that if you fixed the Time Machine, I'd
take you back to see your mom," he said. Wilbur flew
back in time to the night when Lewis was left at the
orphanage.

Lewis saw a woman gently place a baby on the orphanage doorstep. He wanted to say something to her, but he knew it might change his future. He let his chance go by and watched as the woman hurried away.

When they returned to Lewis's time, Wilbur said, "You wanted to meet her so bad. Why'd you just let her go?"

Lewis wasn't sure how to explain. So he simply said, "'cause I'm your dad."

"I never thought my dad would be my best friend," Wilbur confided as he said good-bye. Then he jumped into the Time Machine and blasted off.

Just then, Lewis remembered something. He raced to the baseball field and saw Goob asleep in the outfield.

"Goob! Wake up!" Lewis shouted.

Goob blinked open his eyes—and made the game-winning catch! His future looked bright.

Lewis returned to the science fair, where Dr. Krunklehorn volunteered to try out the Memory Scanner herself. She set a date on the machine. Then after a moment, Dr. Krunklehorn's memories of her wedding day flickered across the screen. Everyone cheered, including the little girl with the box of frogs. Turned out her name was Franny.

Just then, Dr. Krunklehorn's husband, Bud Robinson, arrived to pick up his wife. Winking at Lewis, he said "You don't look like a Lewis. You look more like a—"

"Cornelius!" said Lewis. "I get that a lot."

Dr. Krunklehorn and Bud adopted Lewis. He knew they would be Grandma and Grandpa Robinson one day. They bought a new house with a wonderful room for Lewis to work in. It would become his lab in the future.

At last Lewis had a family. And he knew his future would be bright, just as long as he kept moving forward.